KING BIDGOOD'S IN THE BATHTUB

AUDREY WOOD & DON WOOD

sandpiper

HOUGHTON MIFFLIN HARCOURT

BOSTON   NEW YORK

The text of this book is set in Clearface Roman.
The display text is set in Rococo.
The illustrations are oil on pressed board.

The Library of Congress has cataloged the hardcover edition as follows:
Wood, Audrey.
King Bidgood's in the bathtub.
Summary: Despite pleas from his court, a fun-loving king refuses to get out
of his bathtub to rule his kingdom.
1. Children's stories, American. [1. Kings, queens, rulers, etc.—Fiction.
2. Baths—Fiction.] I. Wood, Don, 1945– ill. II. Title.
PZ7.W846Ki 1985 [E] 85-5472

ISBN: 978-0-15-242730-6 hardcover
ISBN: 978-0-15-242732-0 big book
ISBN: 978-0-15-205435-9 paperback

Manufactured in China
SCP   17 16 15 14
4500686659

For Edwin Cook Brewer

"Help! Help!" cried the Page when the sun came up. "King Bidgood's in the bathtub, and he won't get out! Oh, who knows what to do?"

"I do!" cried the Knight when the sun came up.
"Get out! It's time to battle!"

"Come in!" cried the King, with a boom, boom, boom.

"Today we battle in the tub!"

"Help! Help!" cried the Page when the sun got hot.
"King Bidgood's in the bathtub, and he won't get out!
Oh, who knows what to do?"

"I do!" cried the Queen when the sun got hot.
"Get out! It's time to lunch!"
"Come in!" cried the King, with a yum, yum, yum.

"Today we lunch in the tub!"

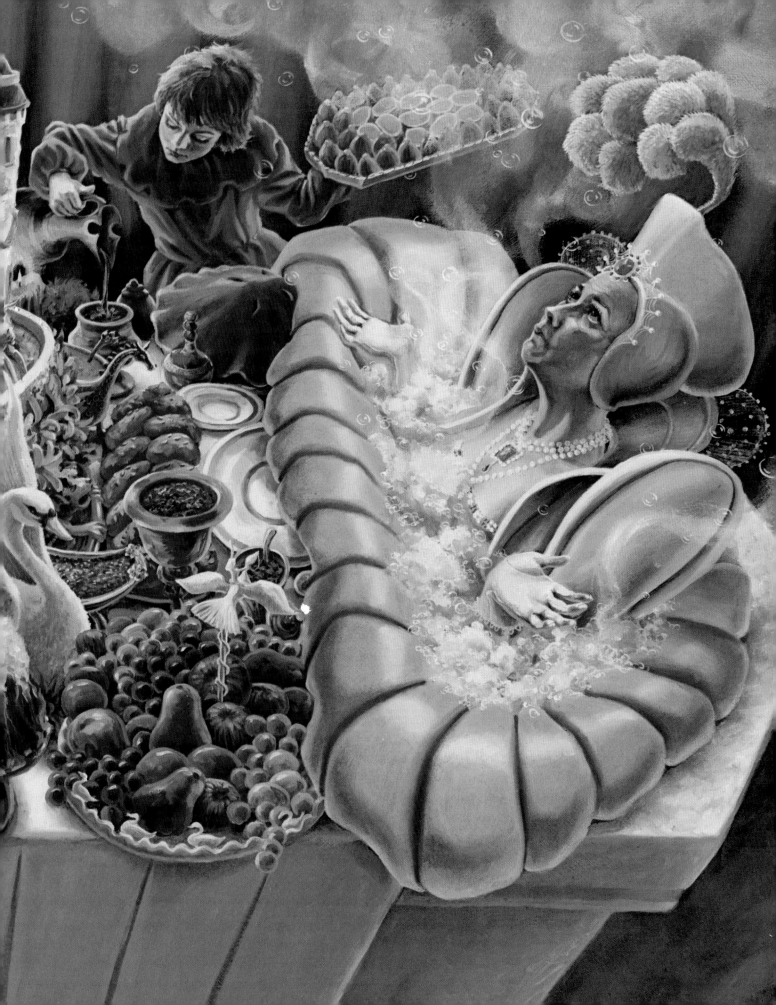

"Help! Help!" cried the Page when the sun sank low.
"King Bidgood's in the bathtub, and he won't get out!
Oh, who knows what to do?"

"I do!" cried the Duke when the sun sank low.
"Get out! It's time to fish!"
"Come in!" cried the King, with a trout, trout, trout.

"Today we fish in the tub!"

"Help! Help!" cried the Page when the night got dark.
"King Bidgood's in the bathtub, and he won't get out!
Oh, who knows what to do?"

"We do!" cried the Court when the night got dark.
"Get out for the Masquerade Ball!"
"Come in!" cried the King, with a jig, jig, jig.

"Tonight we dance in the tub!"

"Help! Help!" cried the Court when the moon shone bright.
"King Bidgood's in the bathtub, and he won't get out!
Oh, who knows what to do?
Who knows what to do?"

"I do!" said the Page when the moon shone bright,
and then he pulled the plug.

Glub, glub, glub!